PROVERBS 3
I AM STATEMENTS

I am a woman of **Noble Character**

I am trustworthy and my value is far above rubies

I am diligent in my work and bring good to my family

I am joyfully engaged in the tasks of my home

I am wise and provide instruction with kindness

I am strong and honor my responsibilities

I am clothed in strength and dignity

I am a source of laughter and do not fear the future

I am filled with wisdom and the fear of the LORD

I am a blessing to those around me

I am celebrated for my achievements and my heart of service

I am a source of inspiration for future generations

Copyright 2024 by Nakia Knowles
No part of this book may be used or
reproduced in any manner whatsoever
without prior written permission of the author
Nakia Knowles except for the use of
brief quotations in a book review

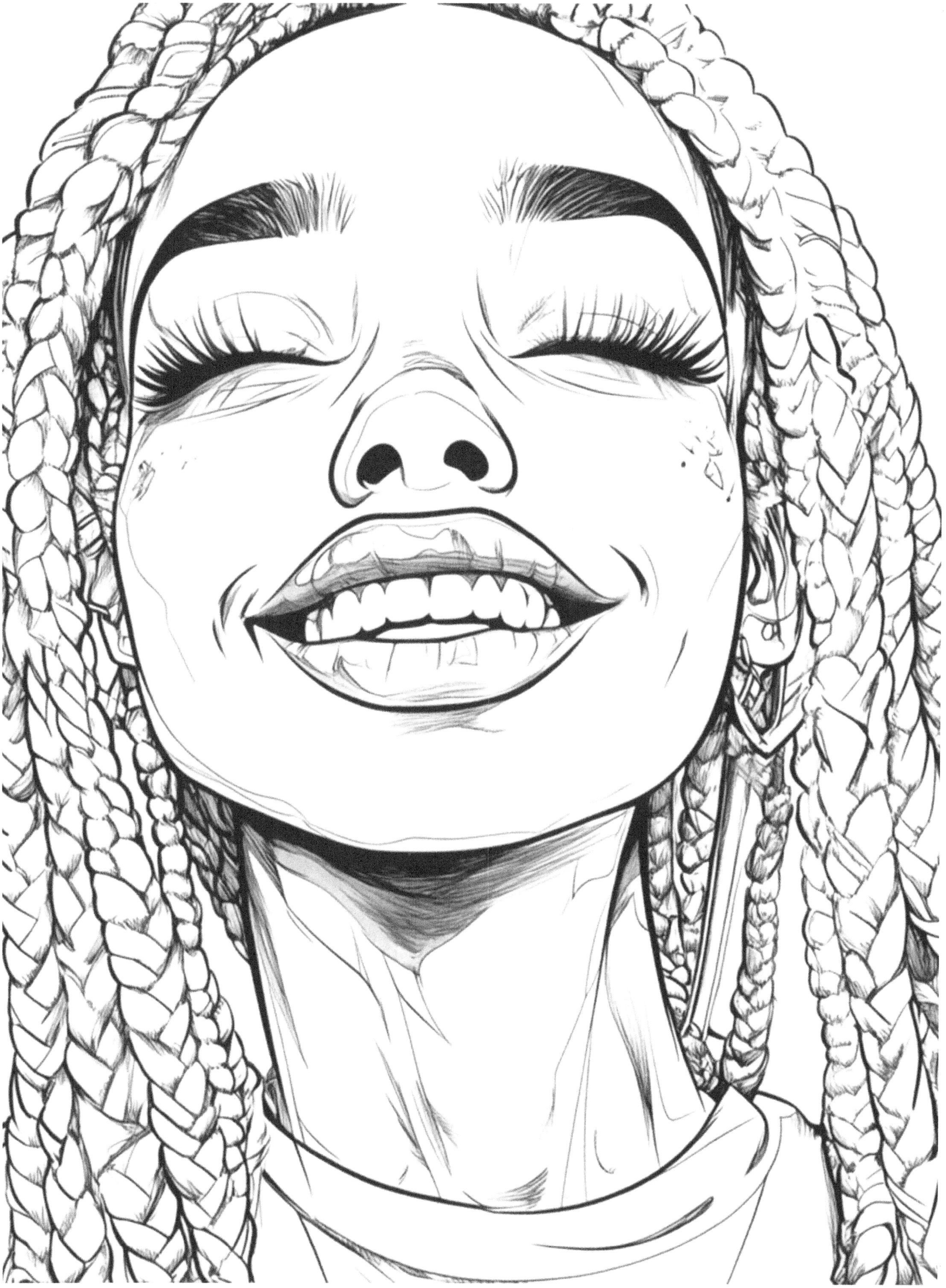

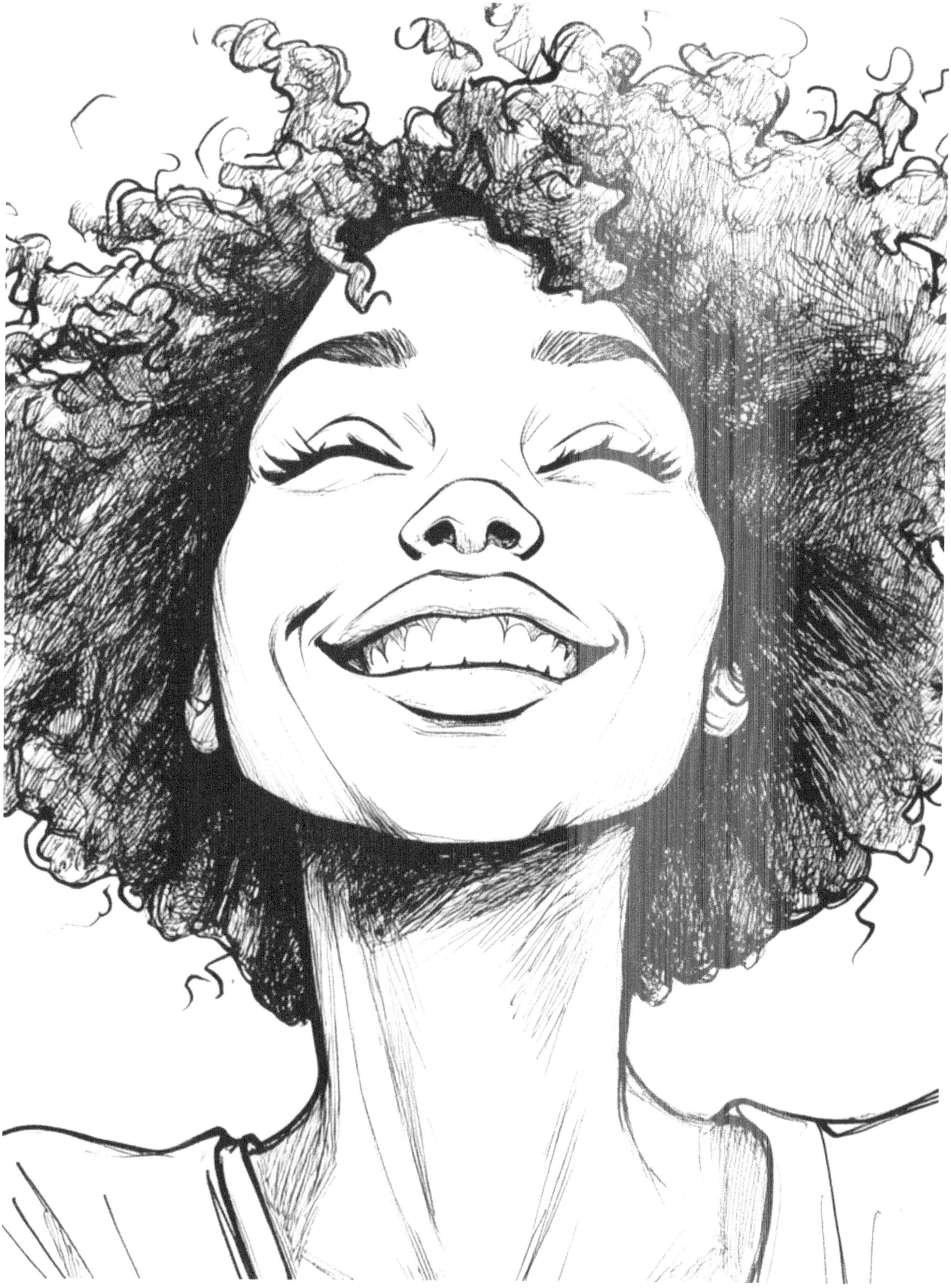

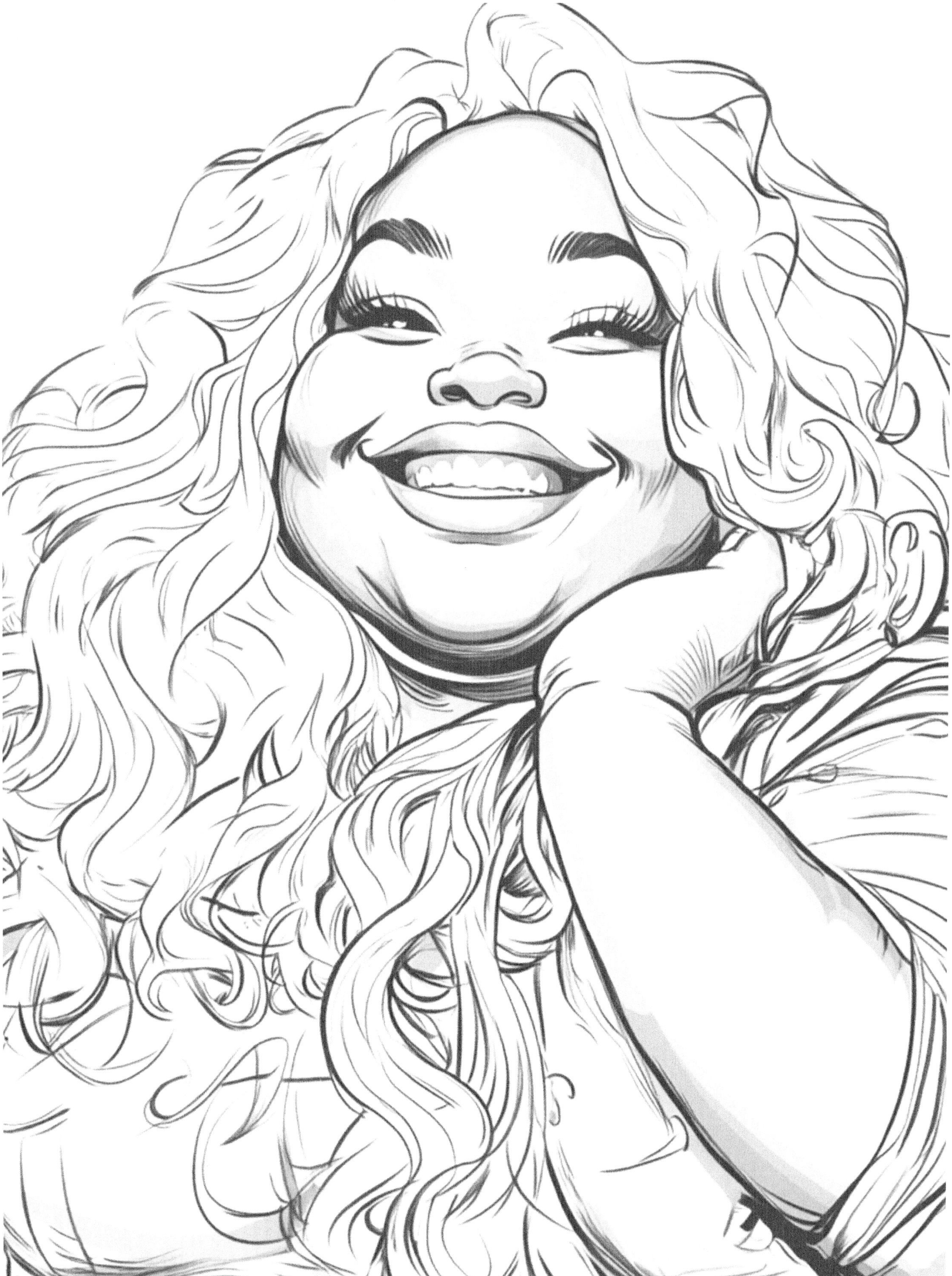

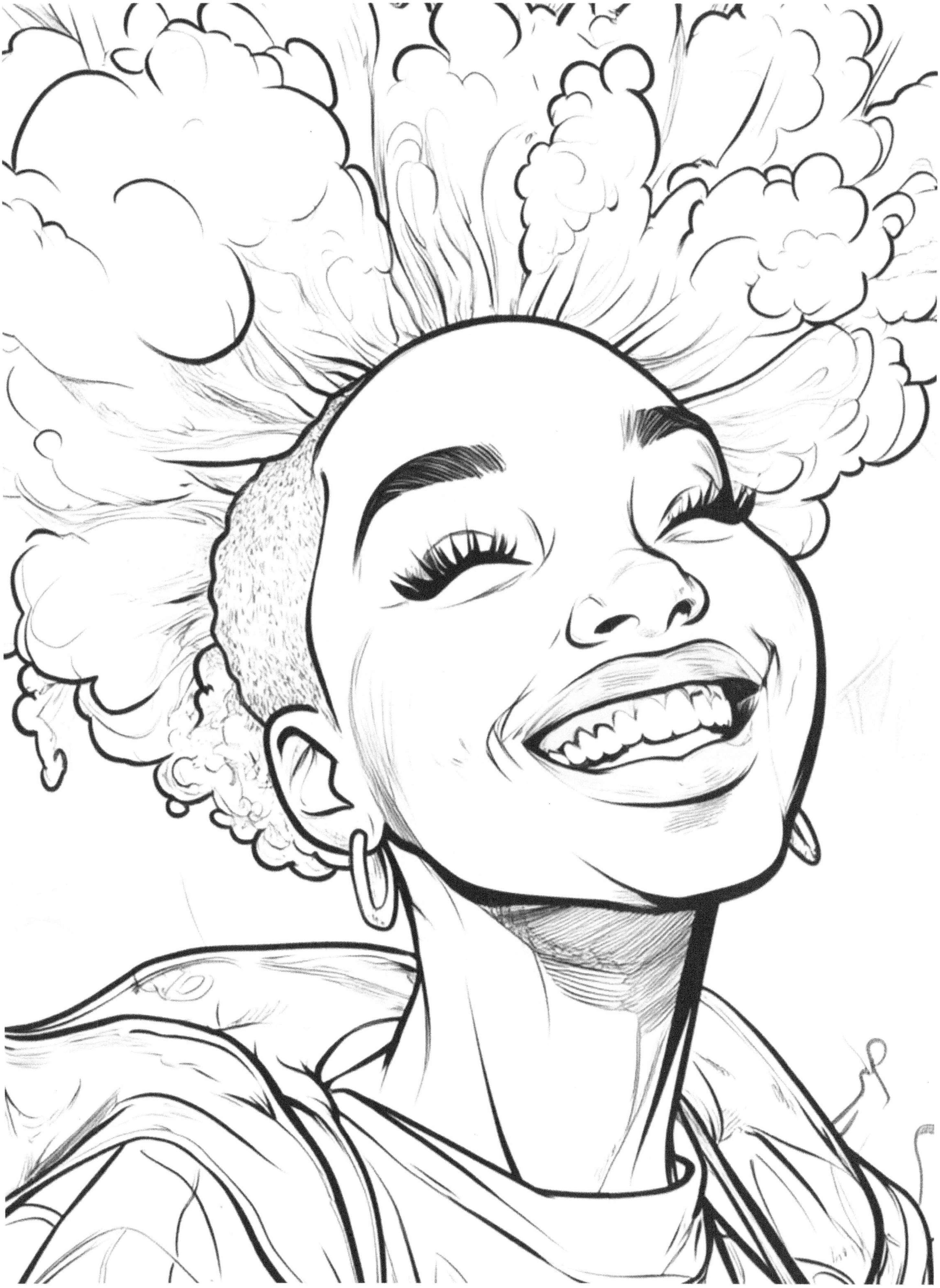

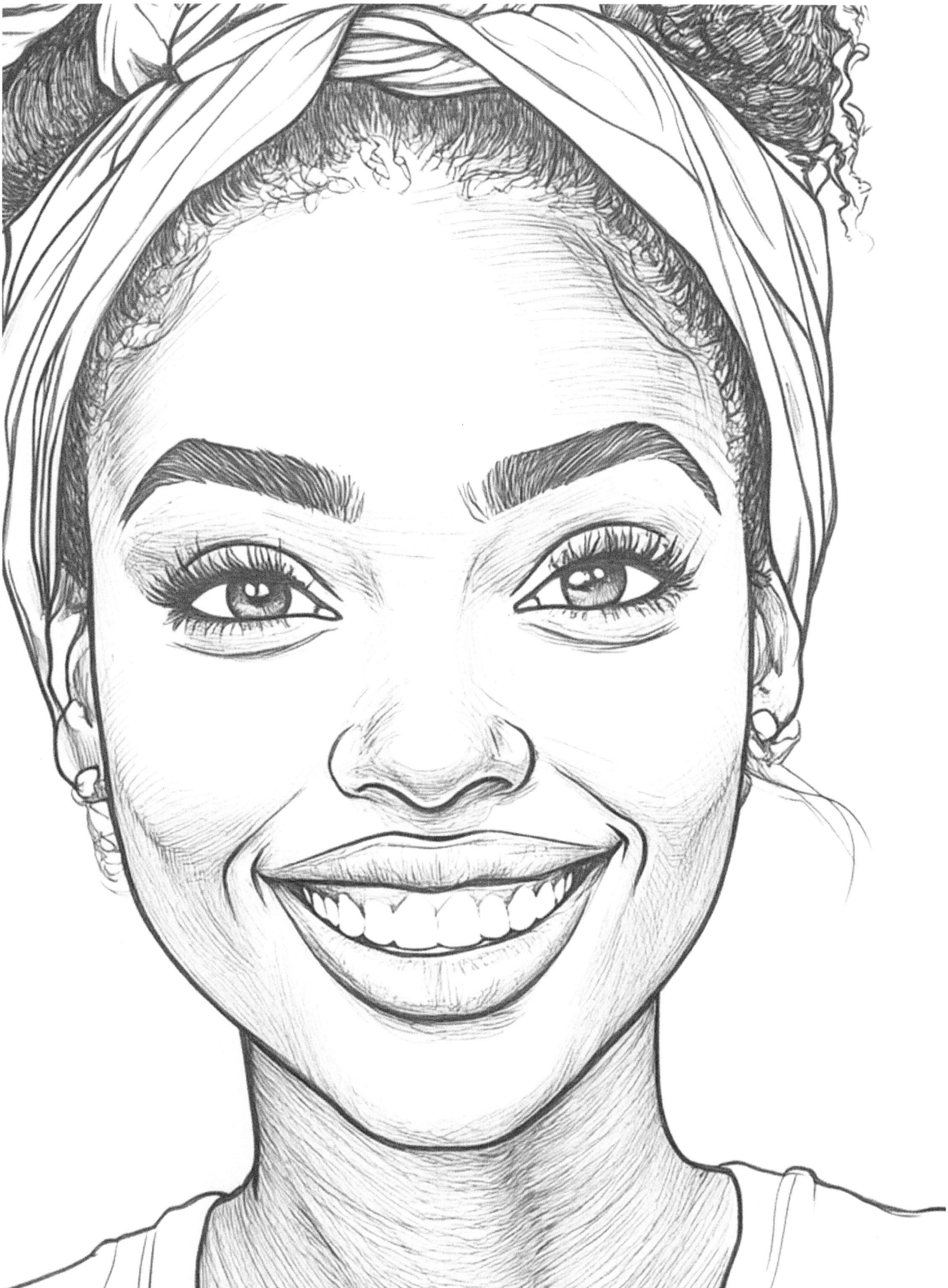

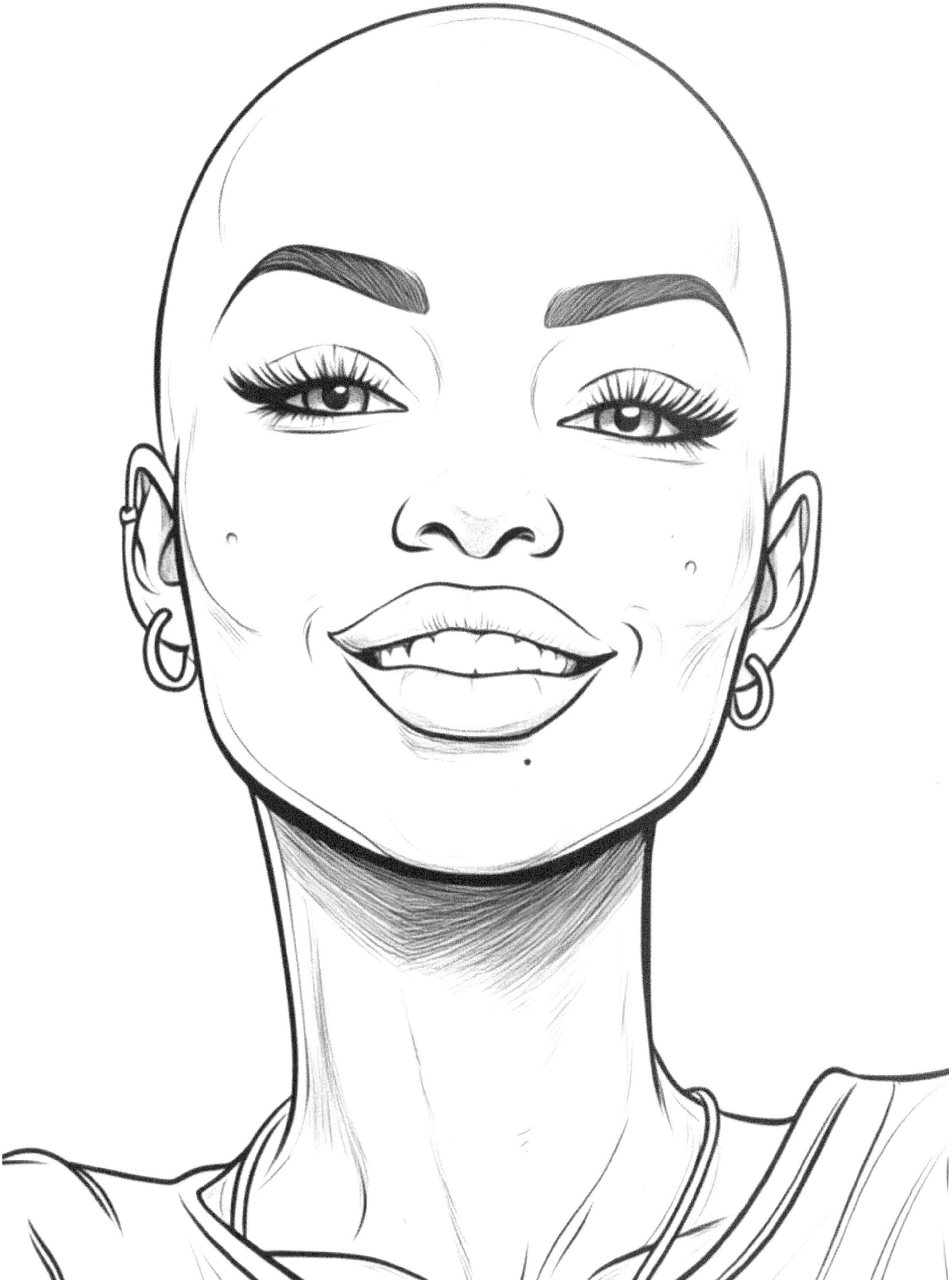

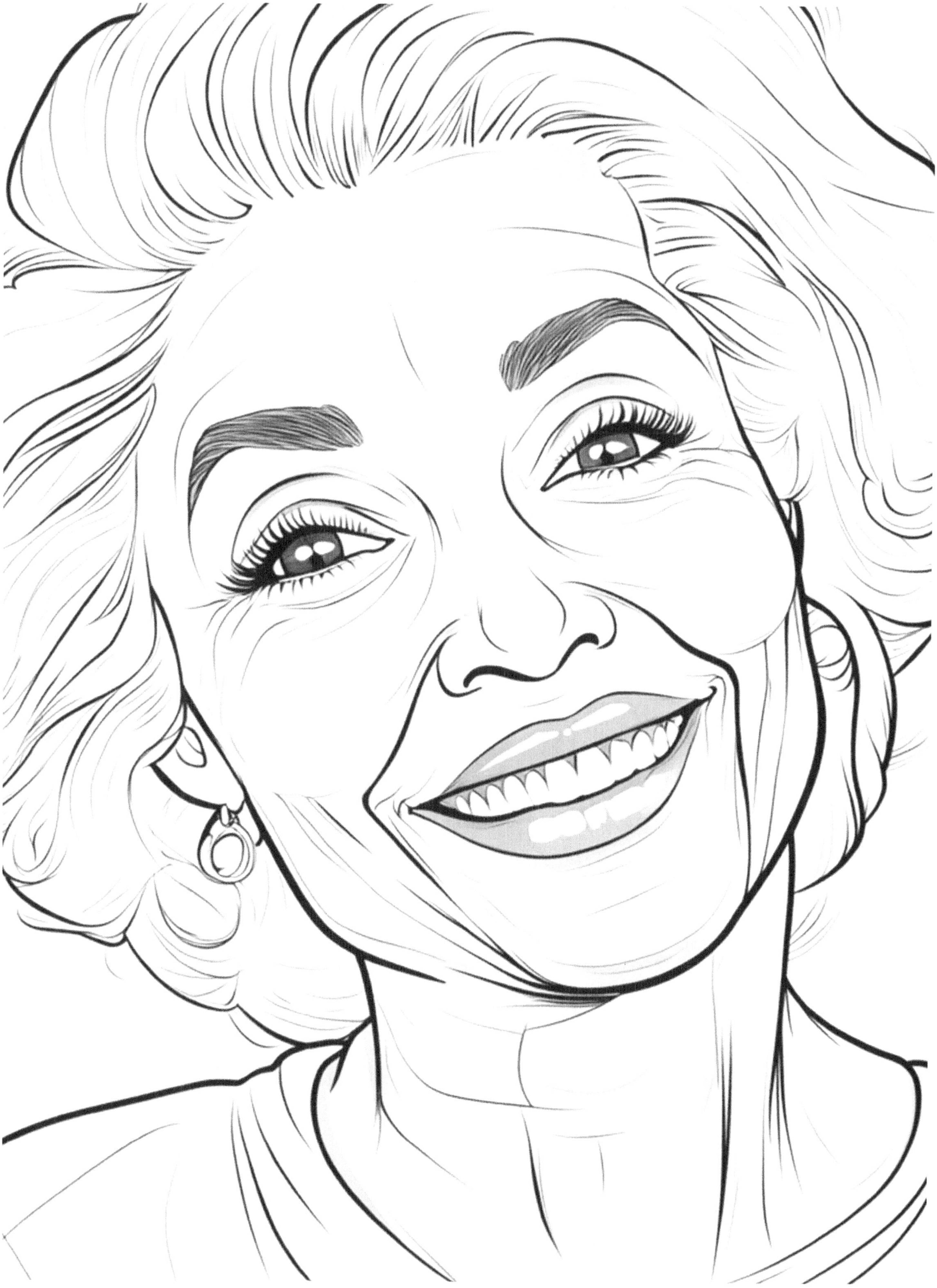

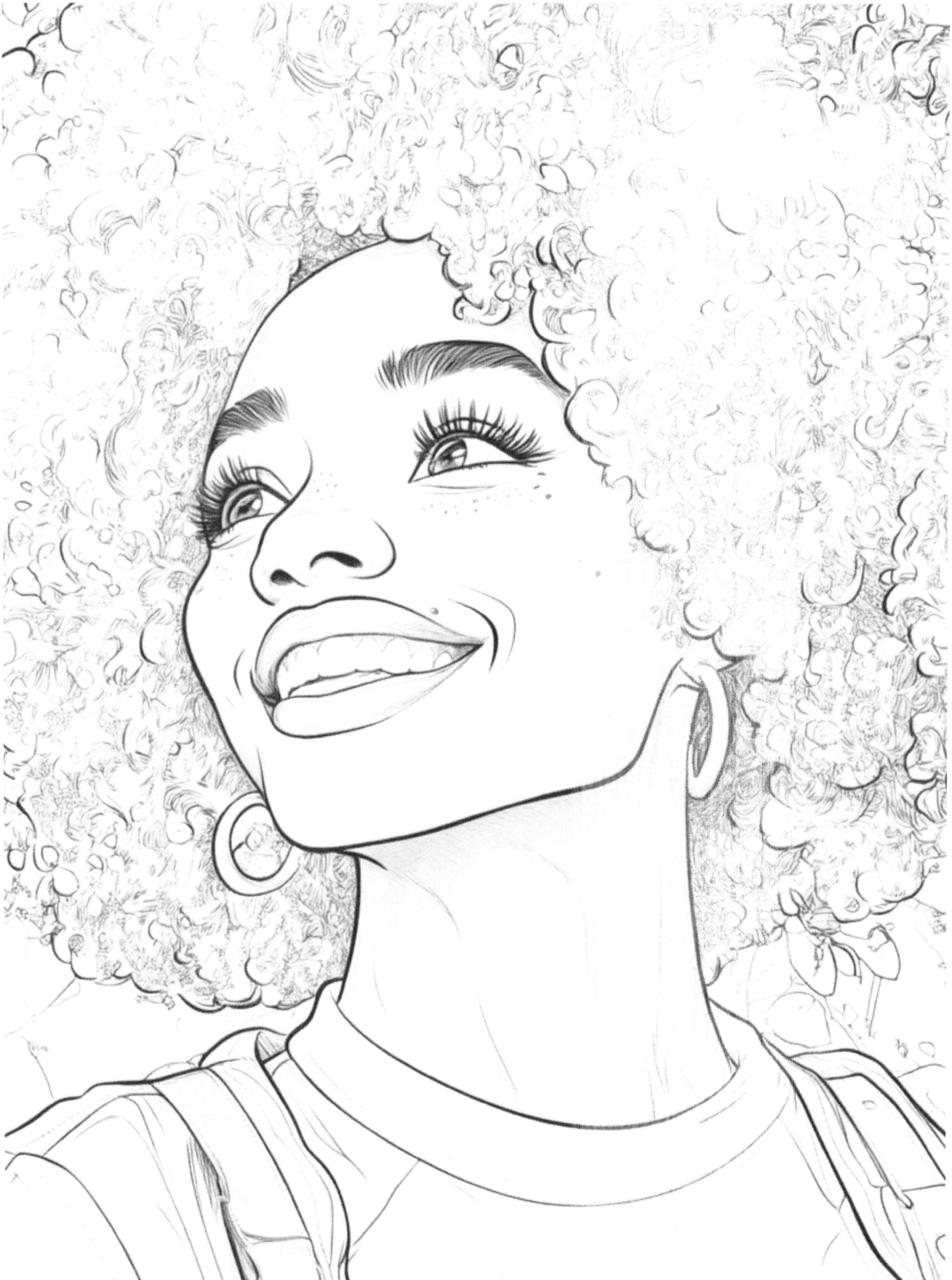

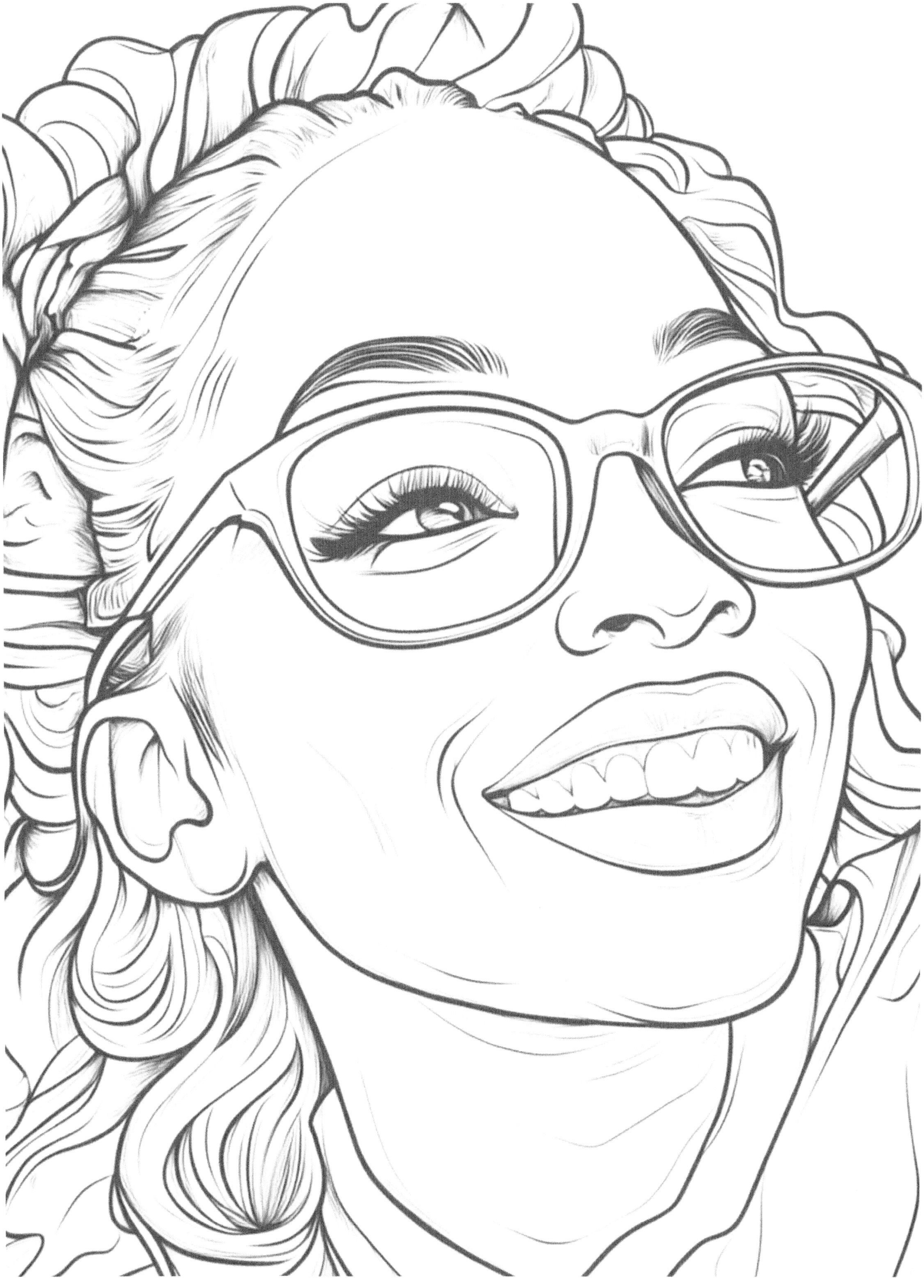

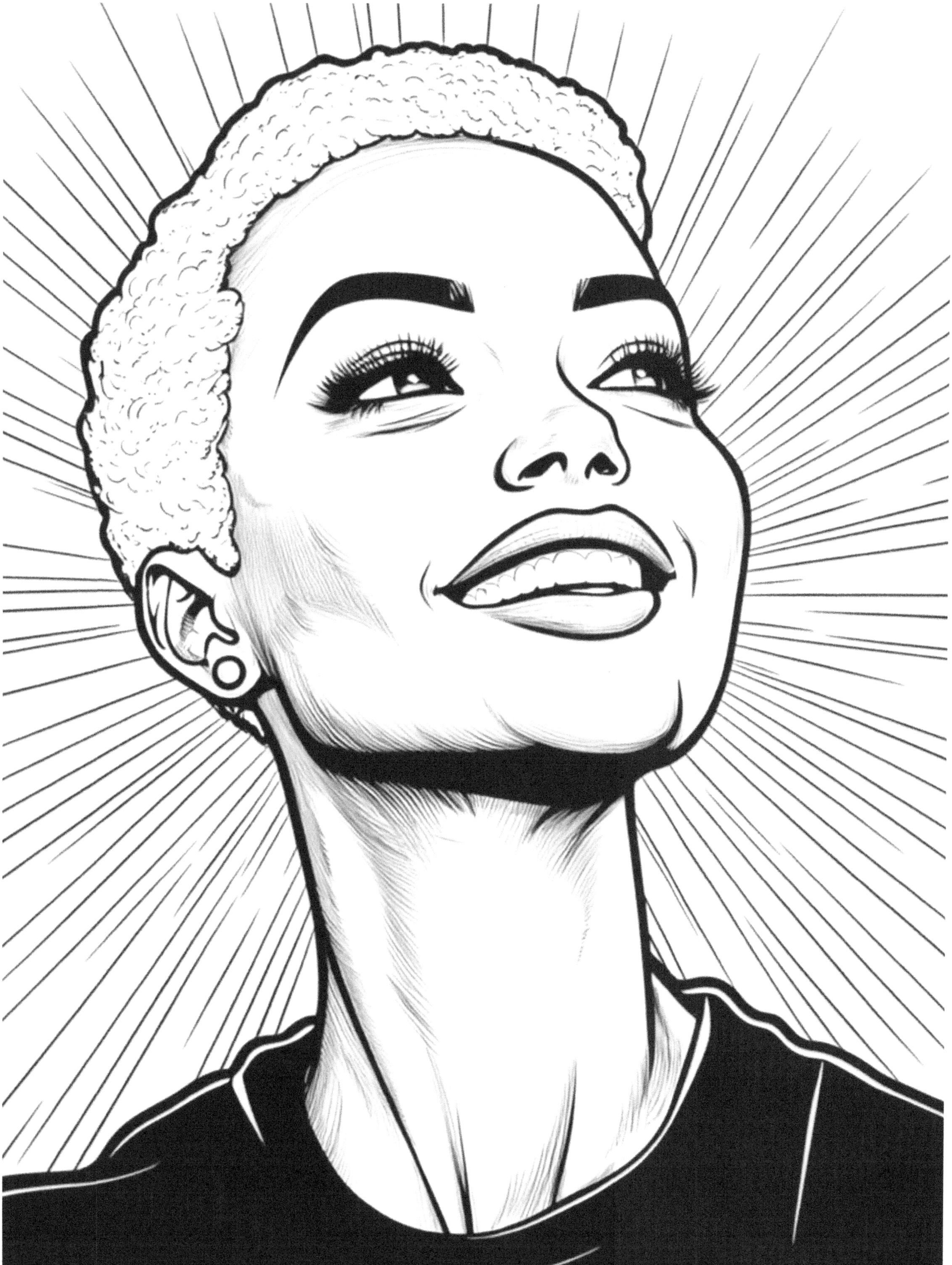

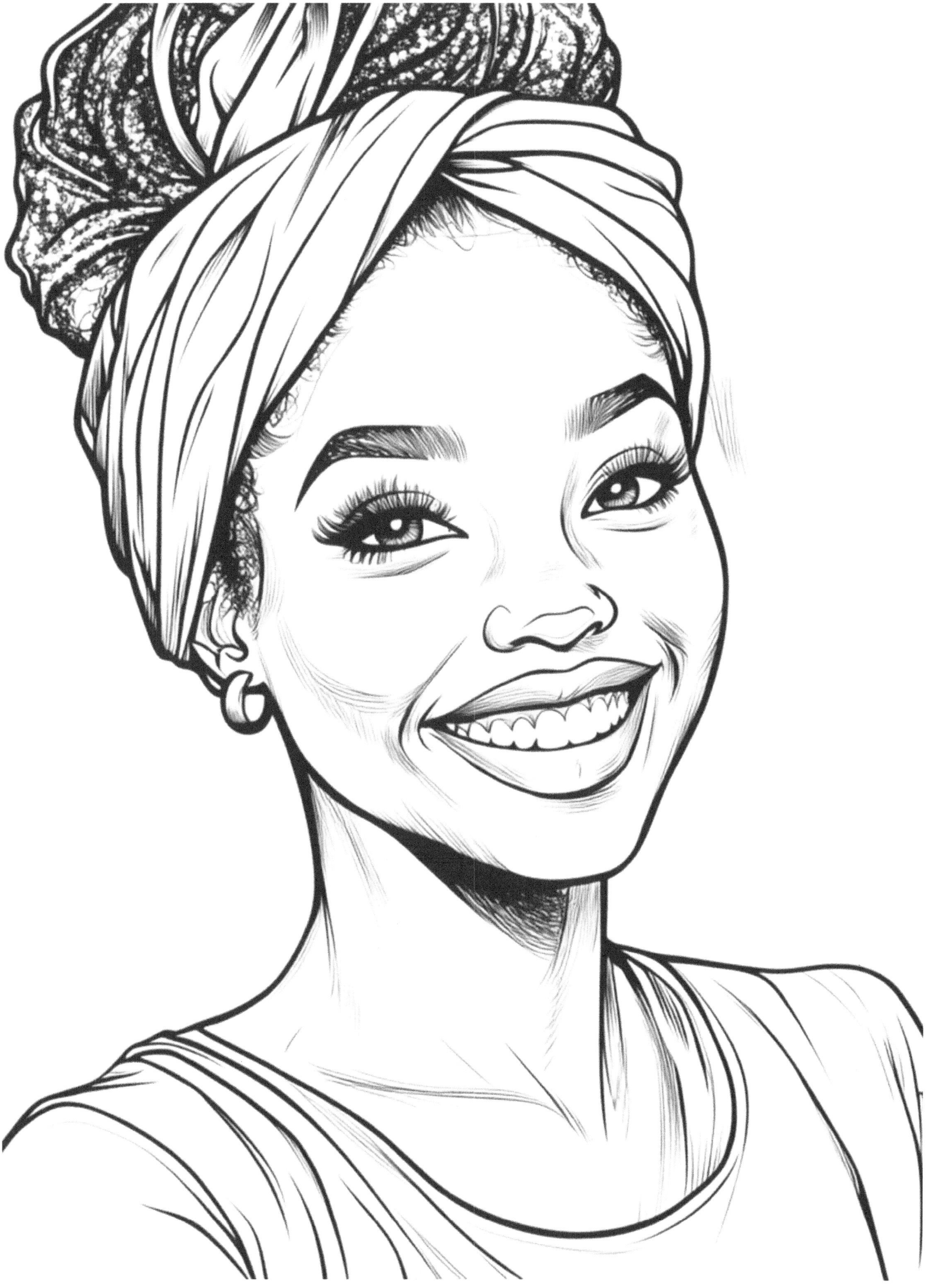

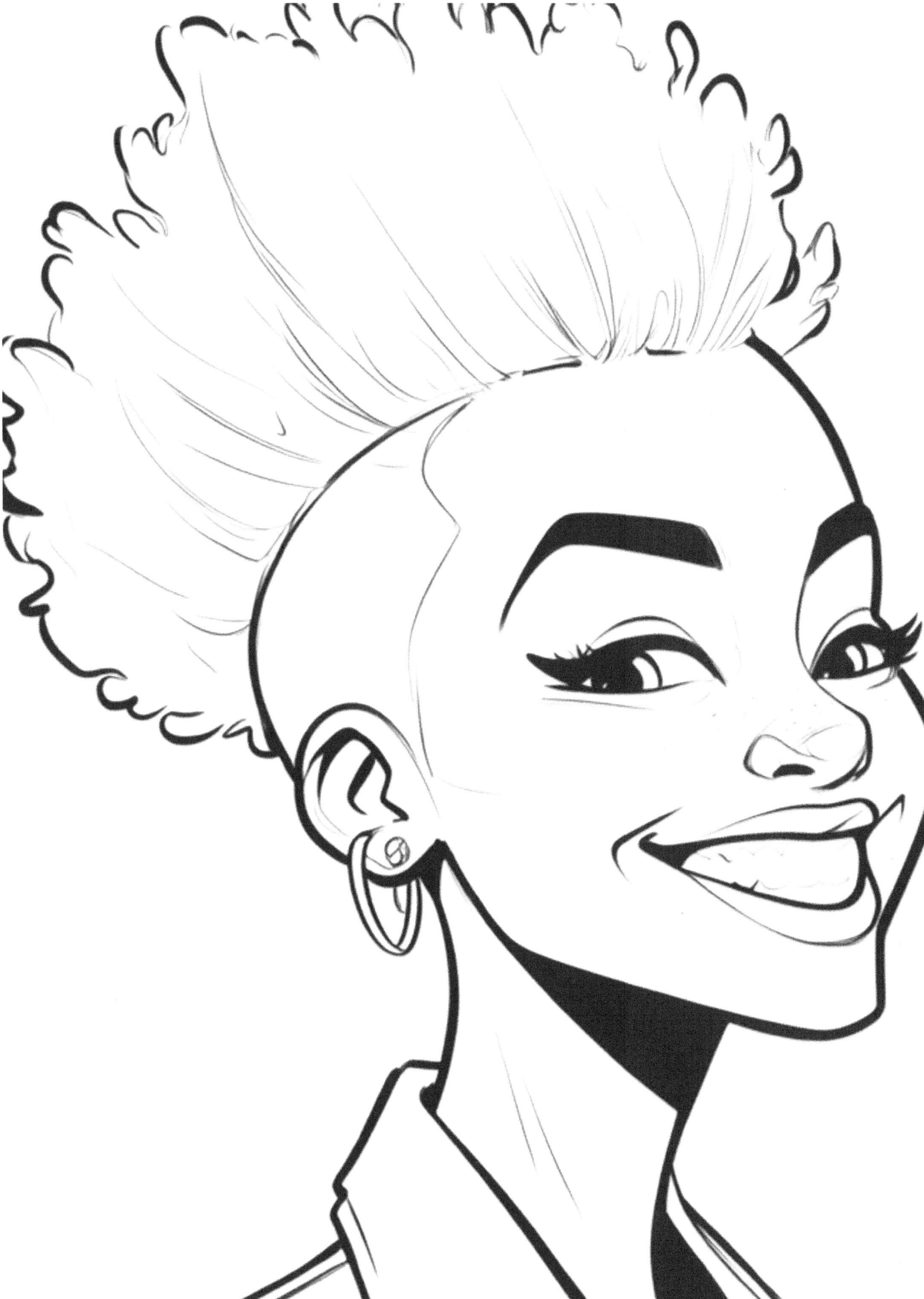

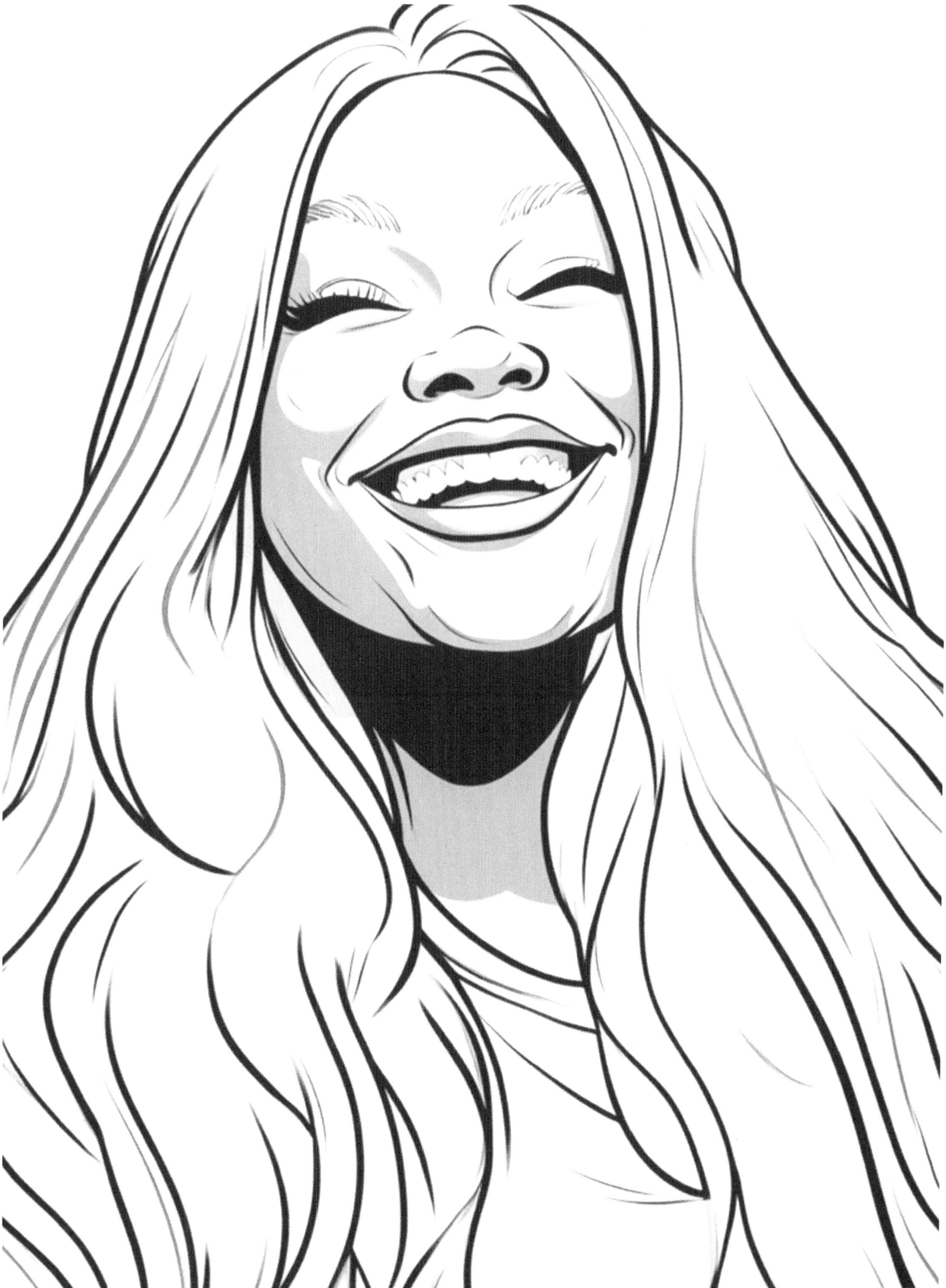

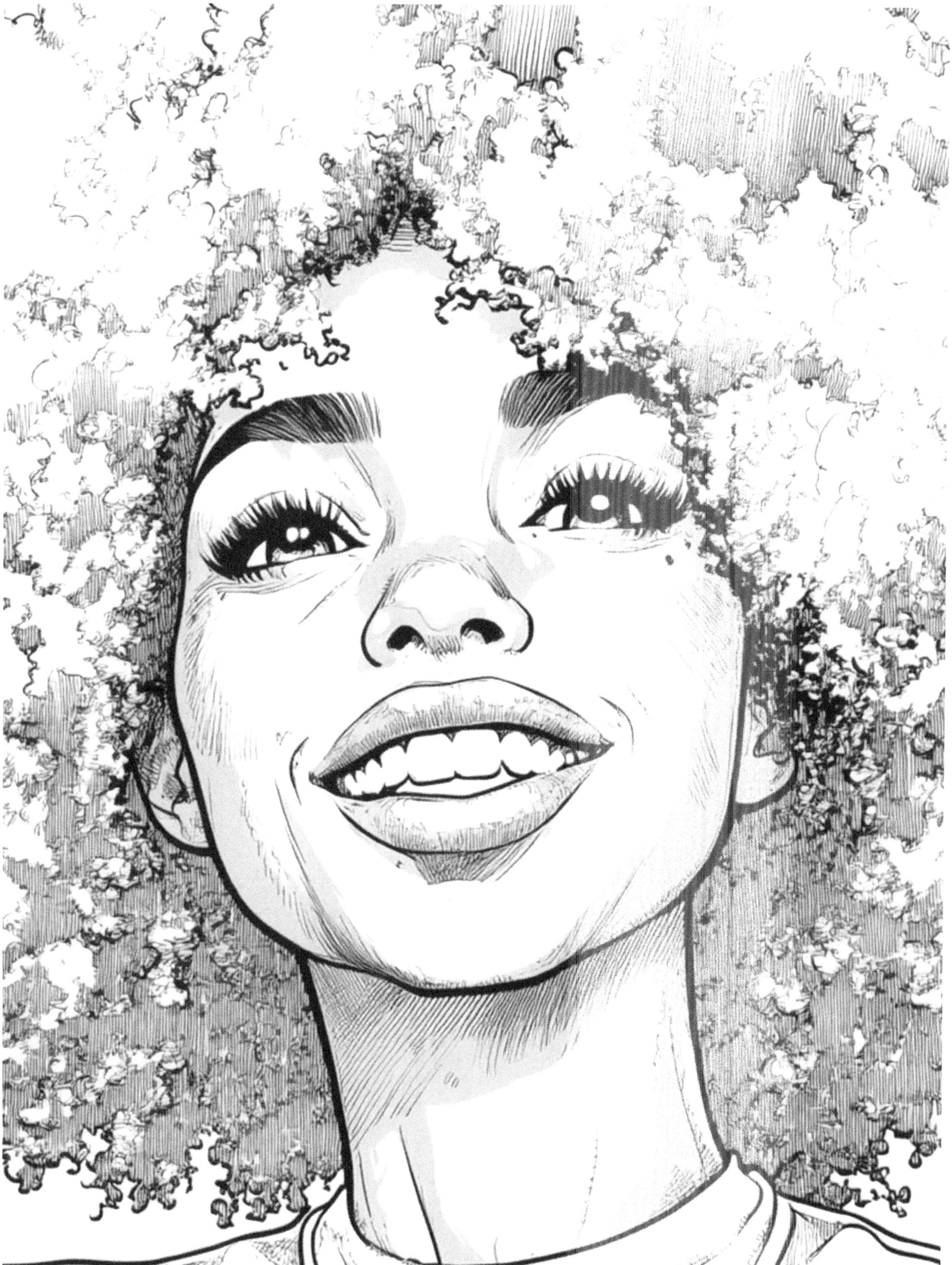

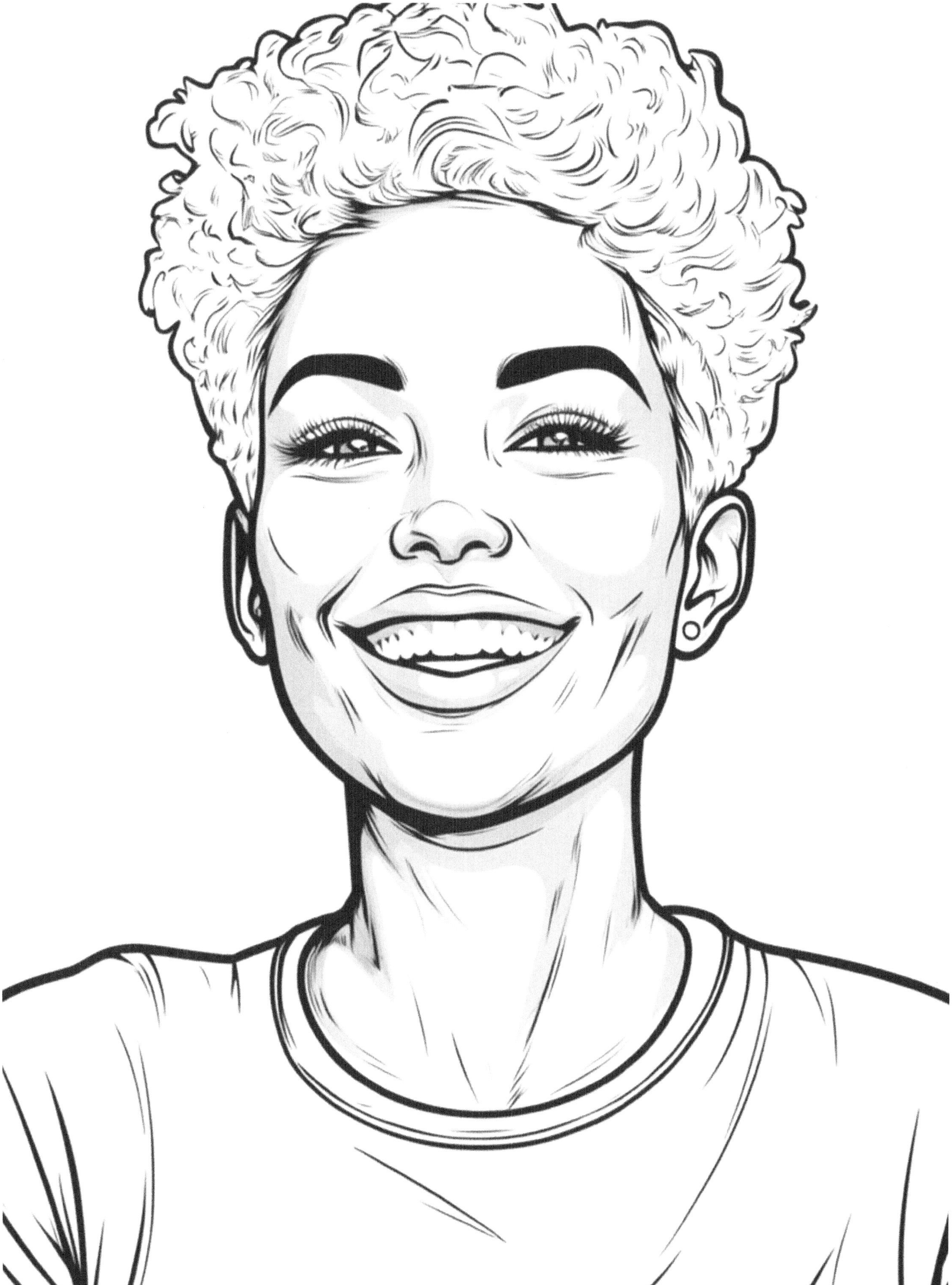

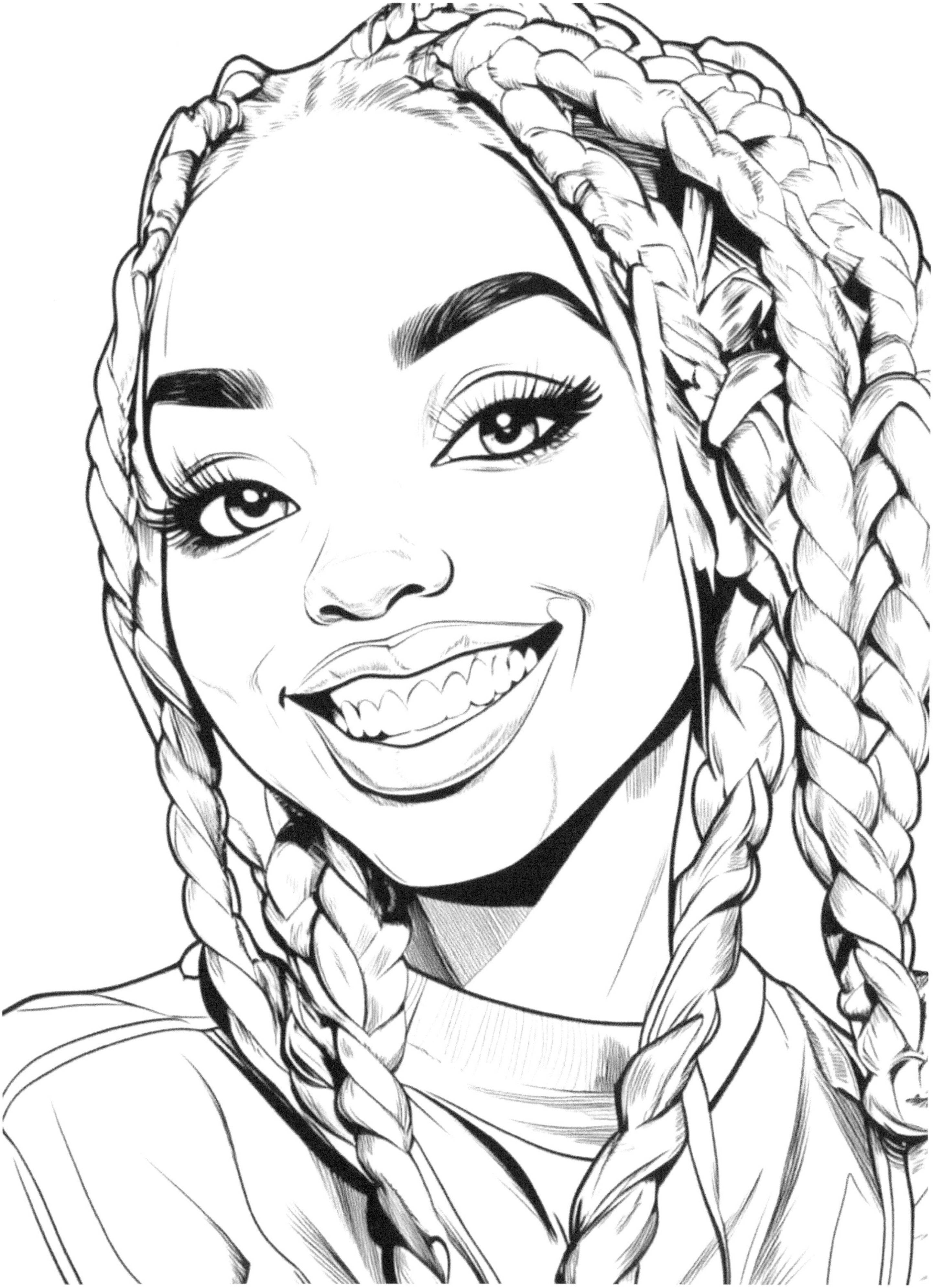

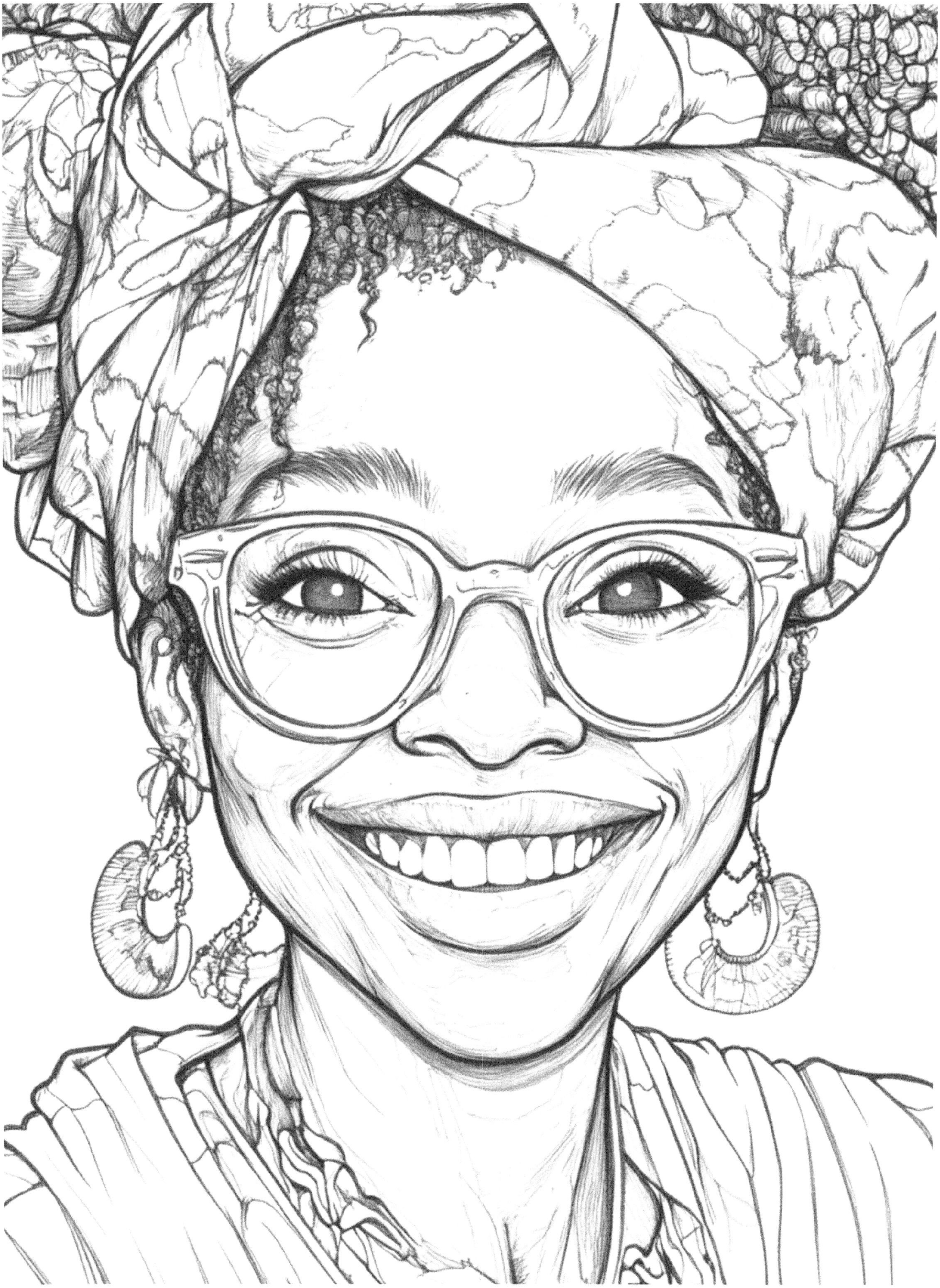

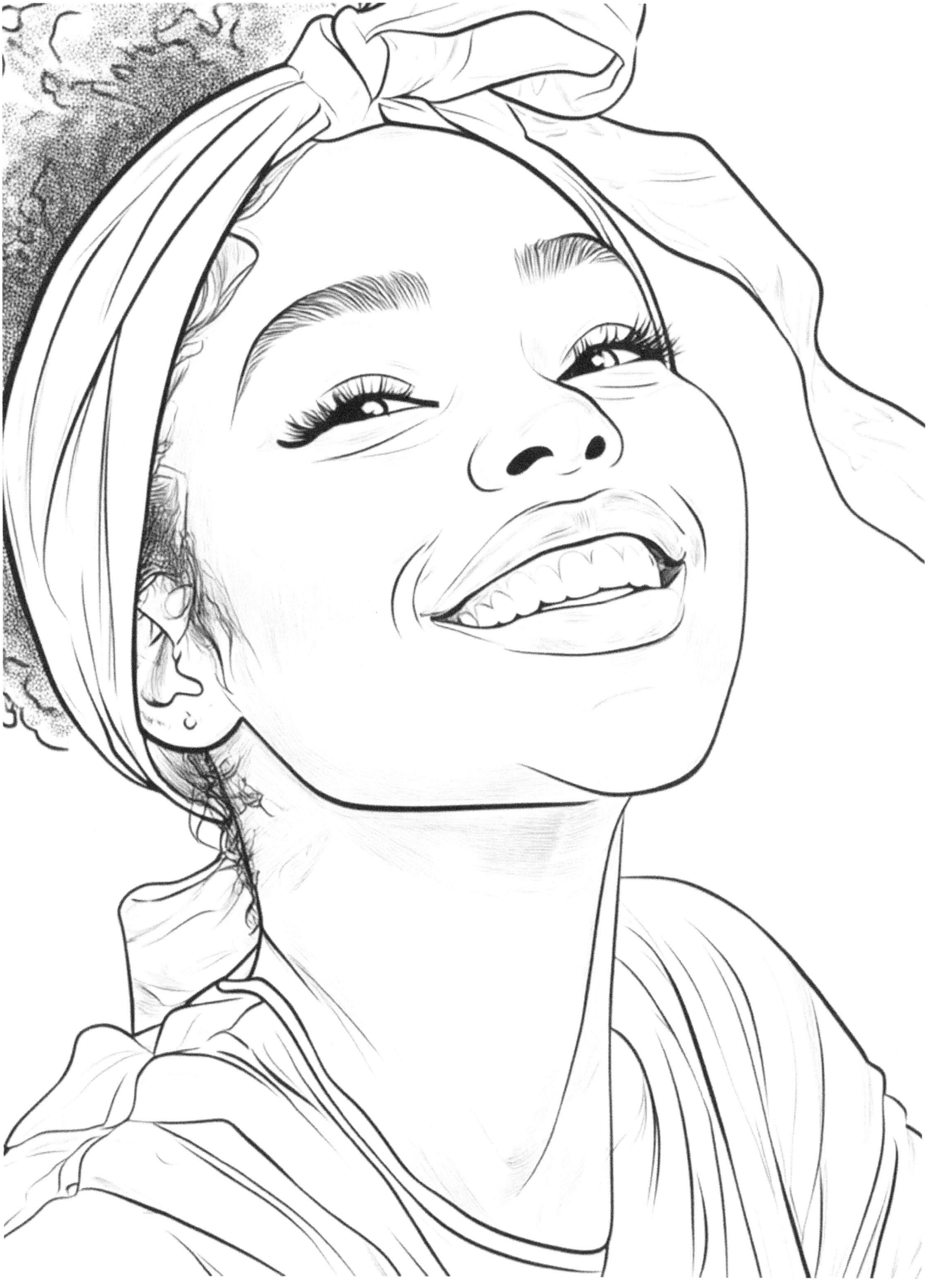

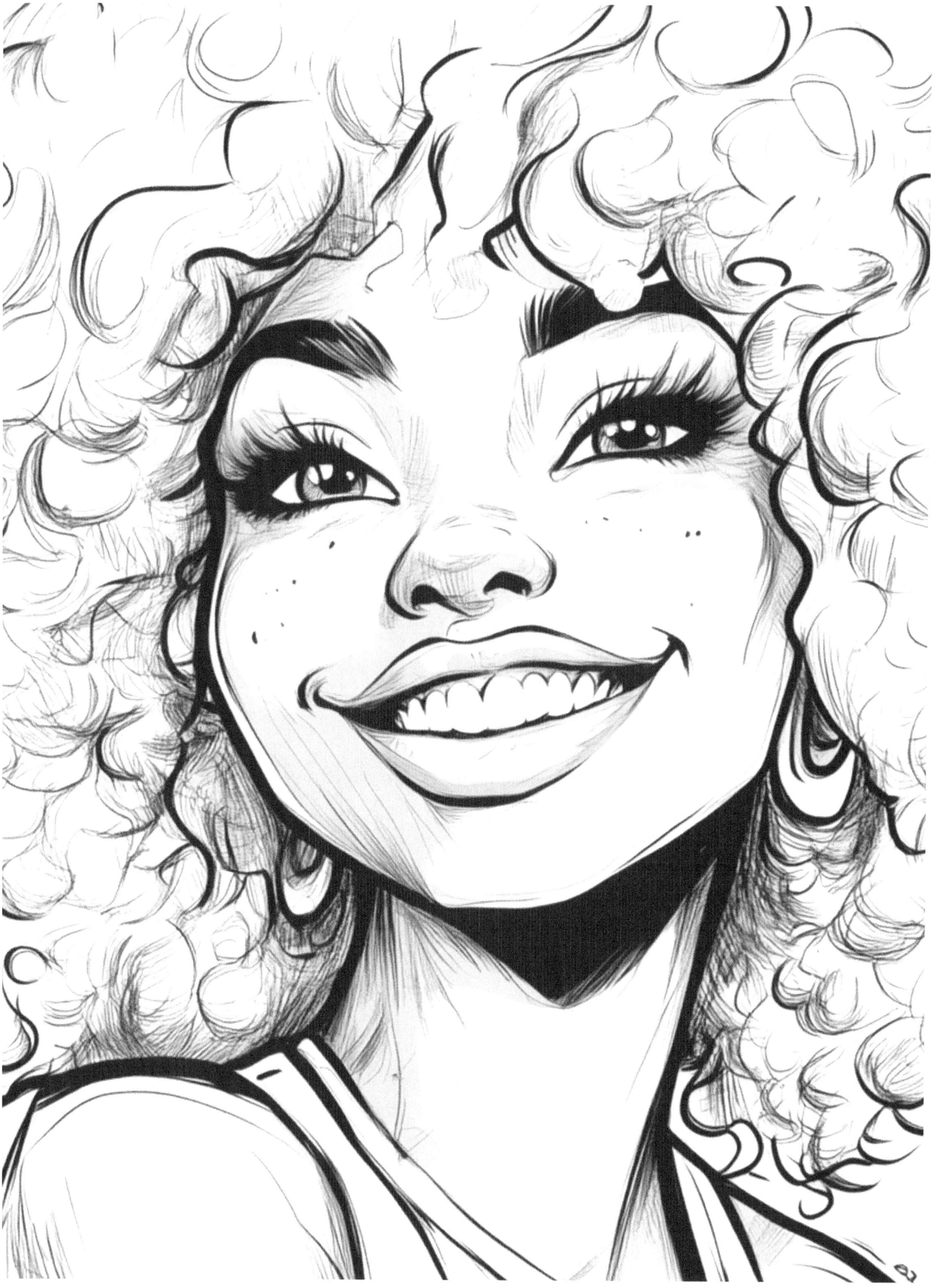

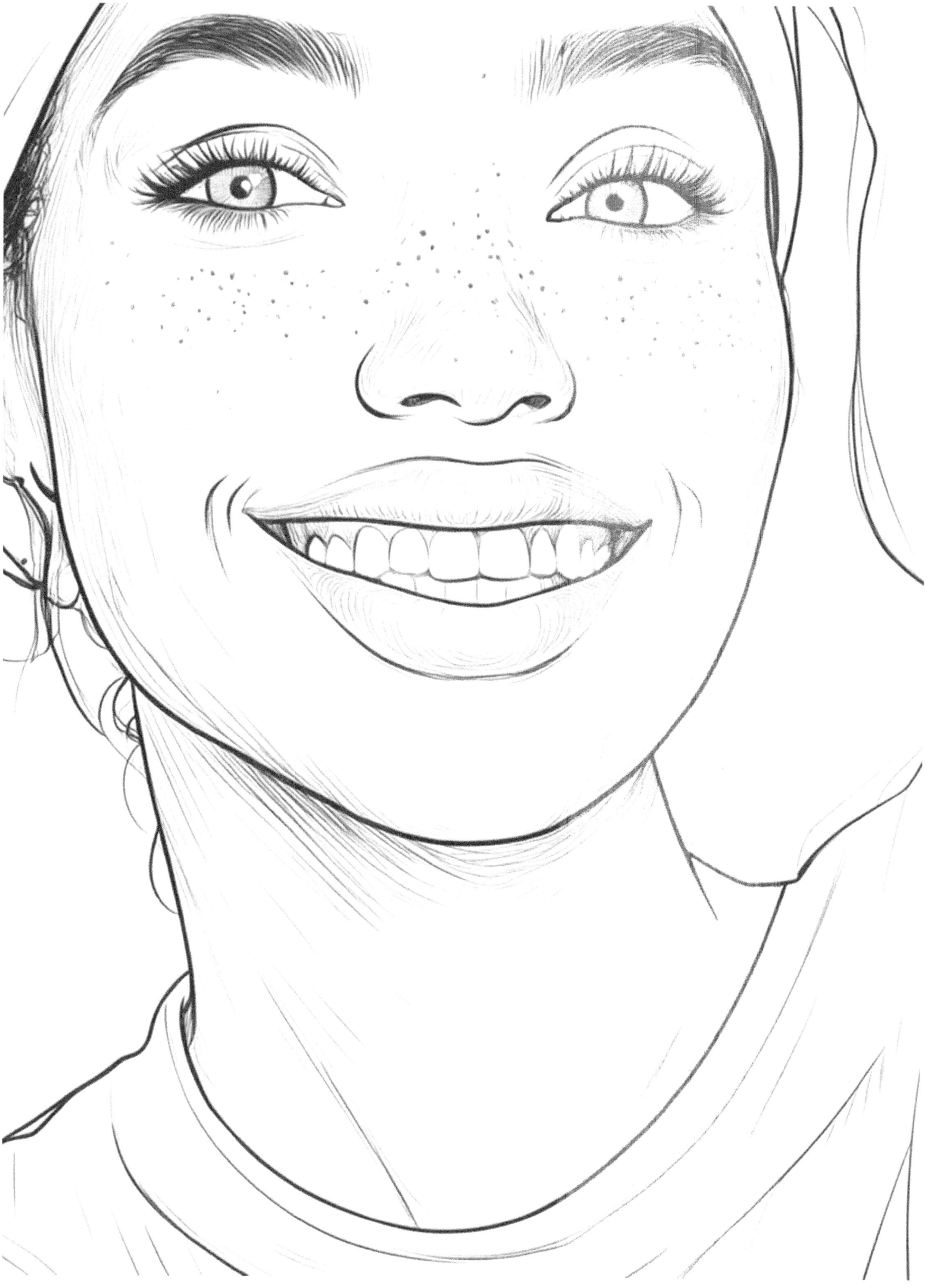

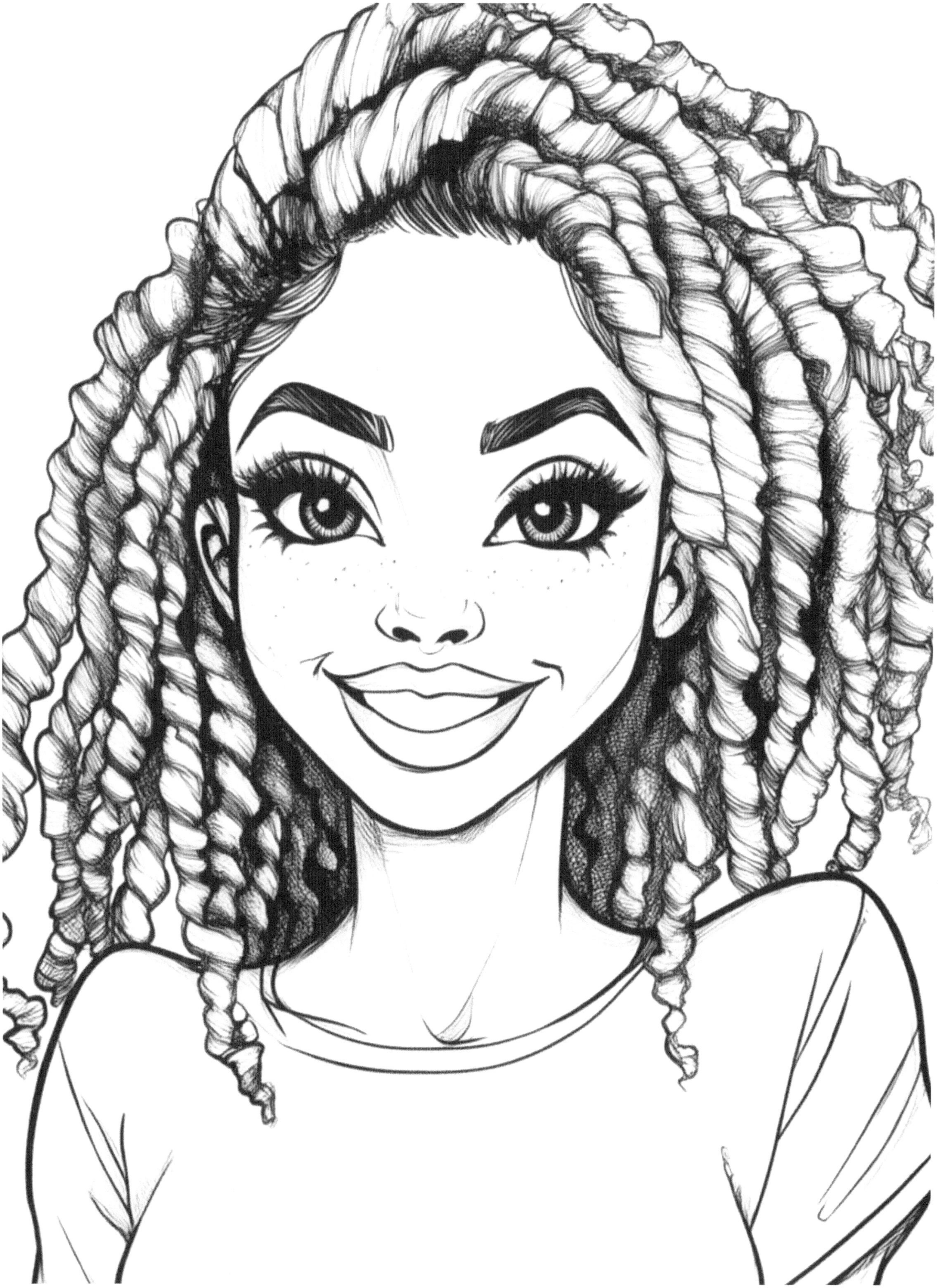

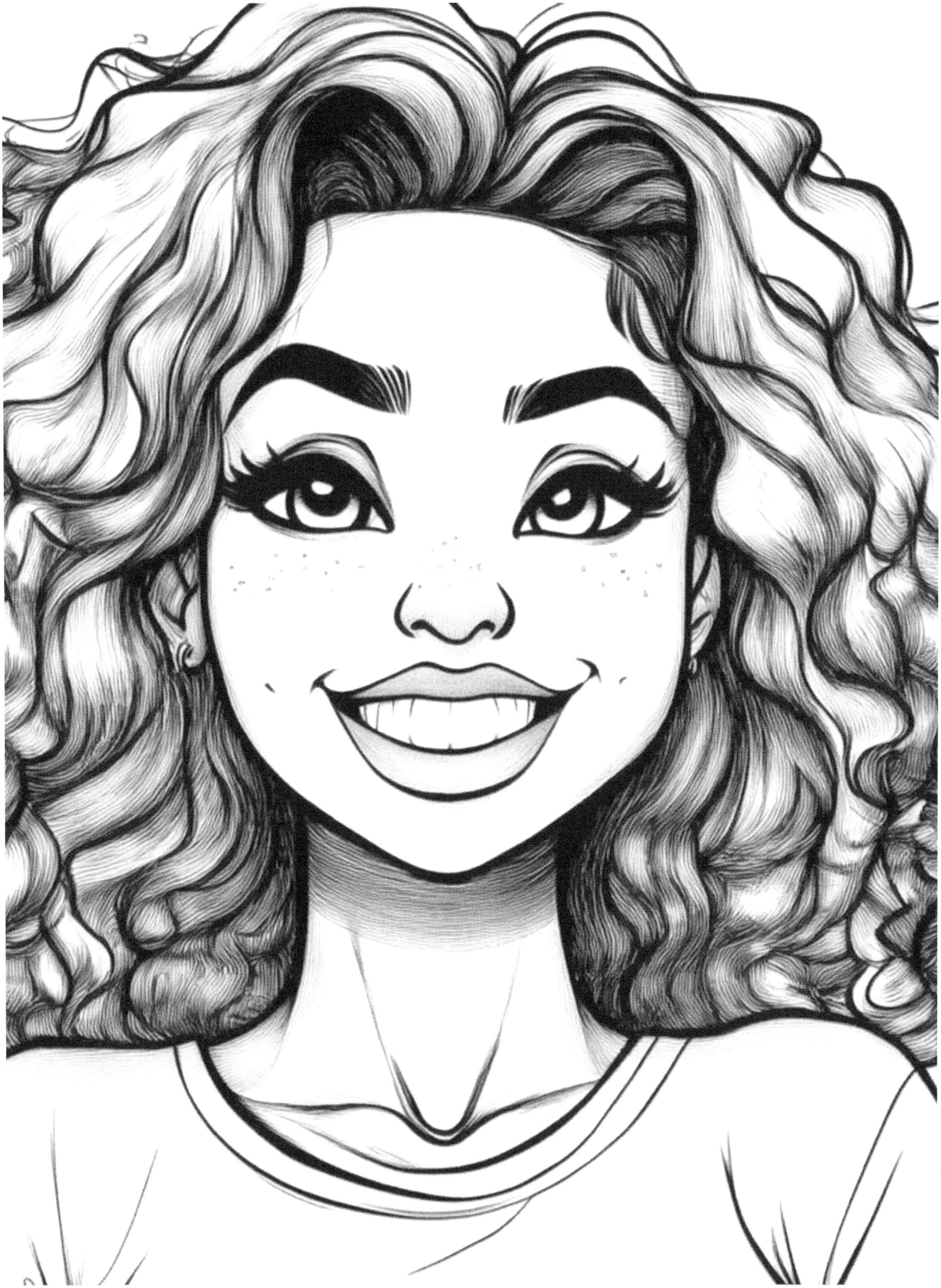

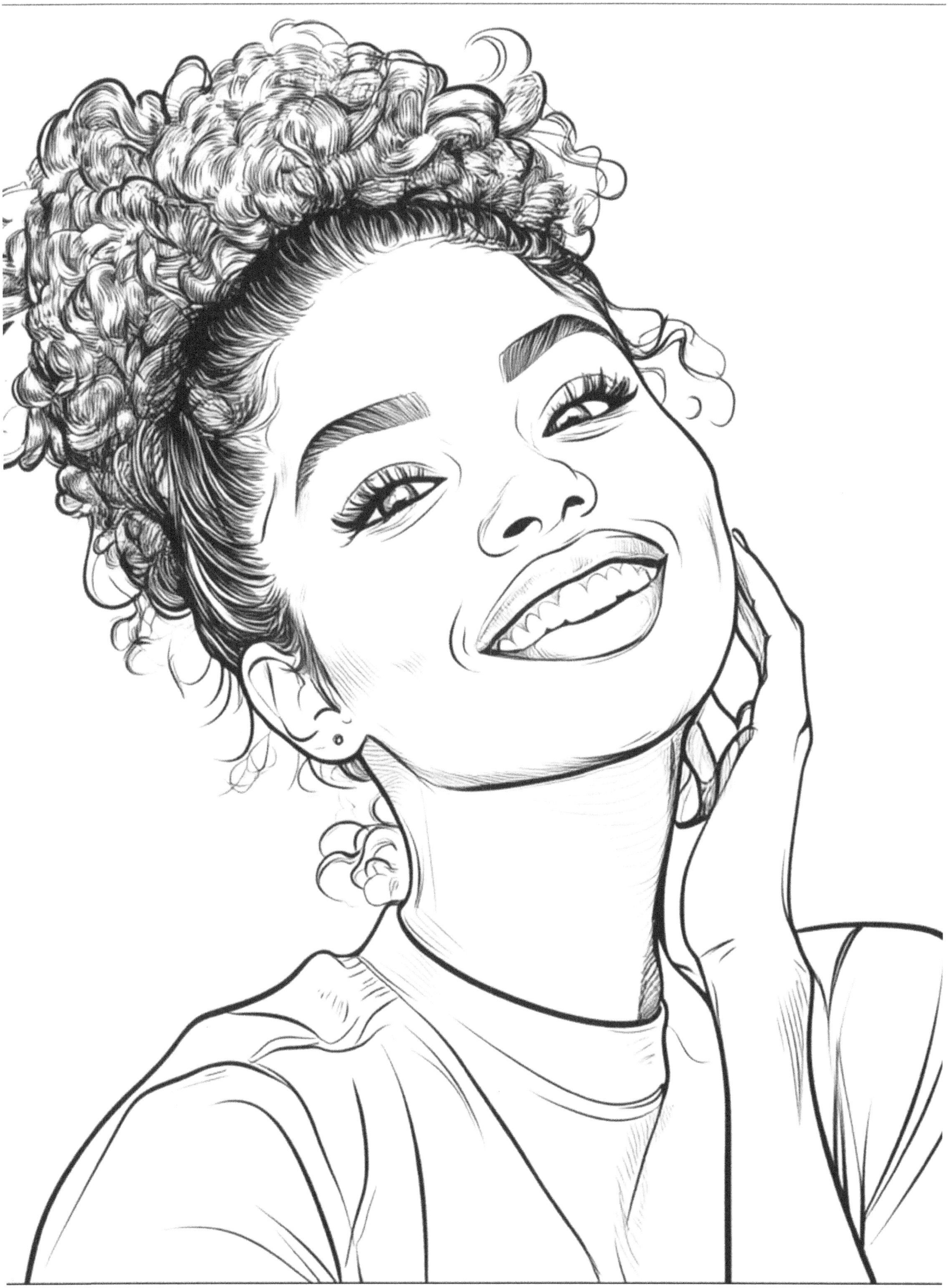

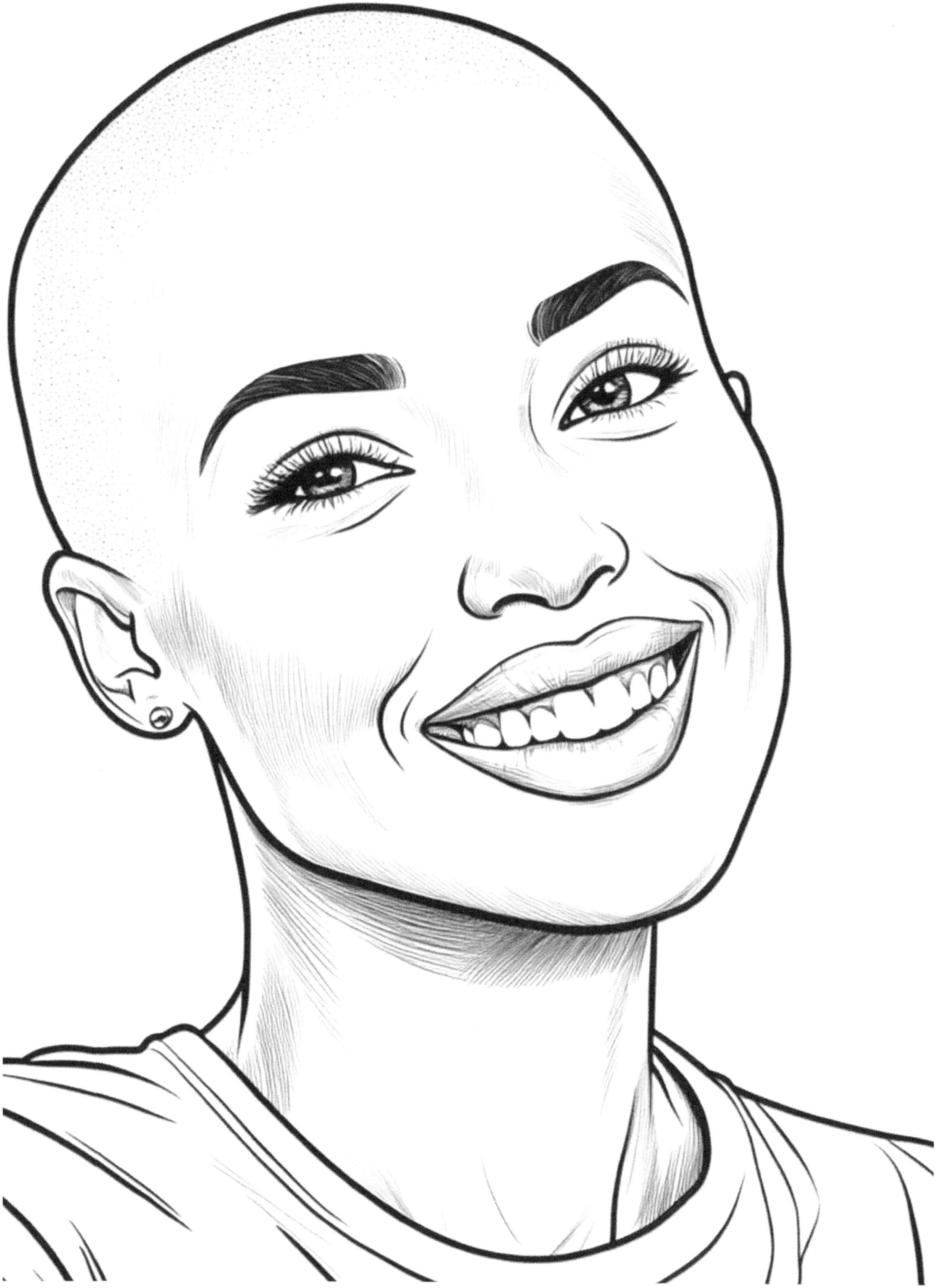

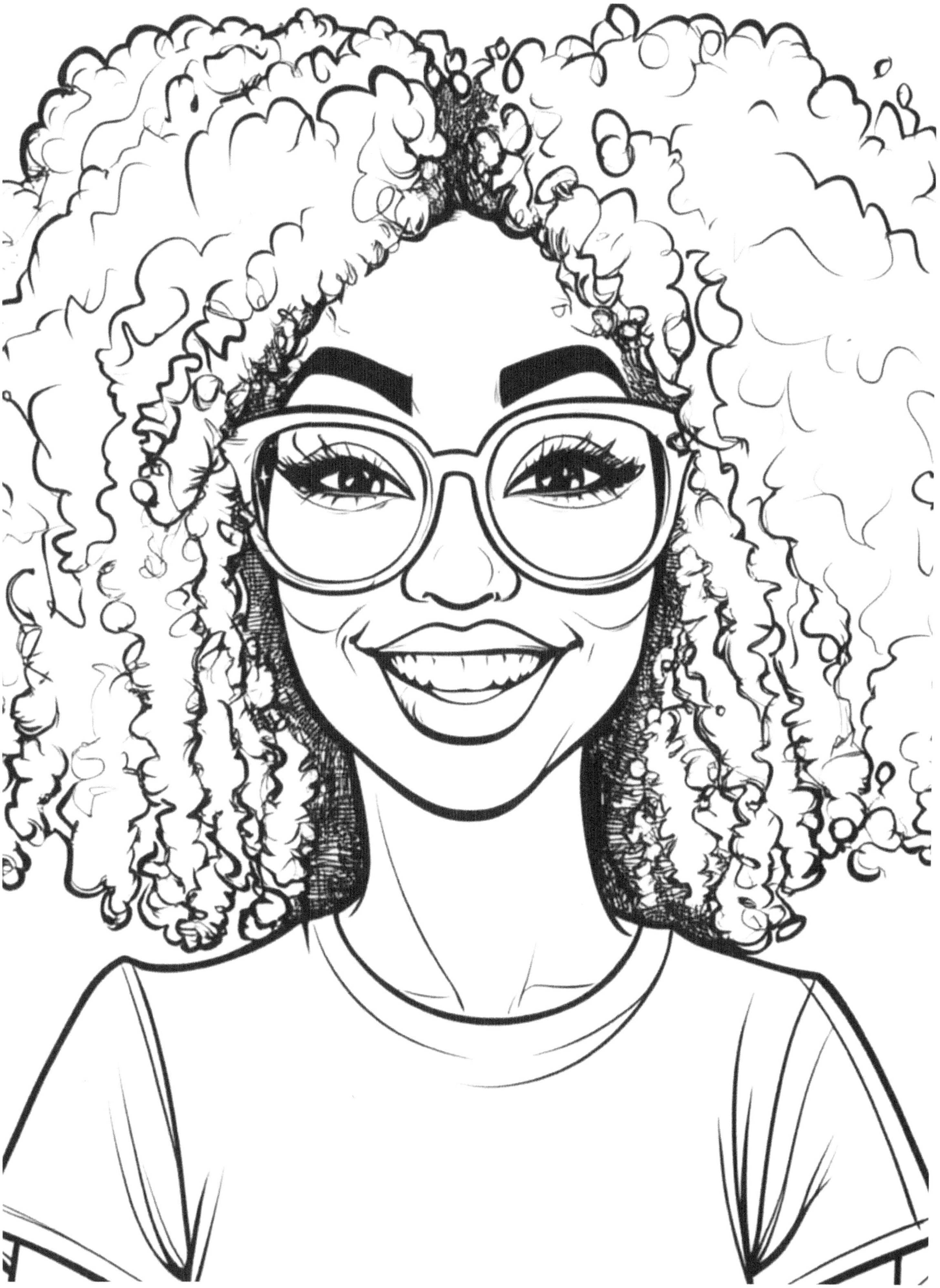

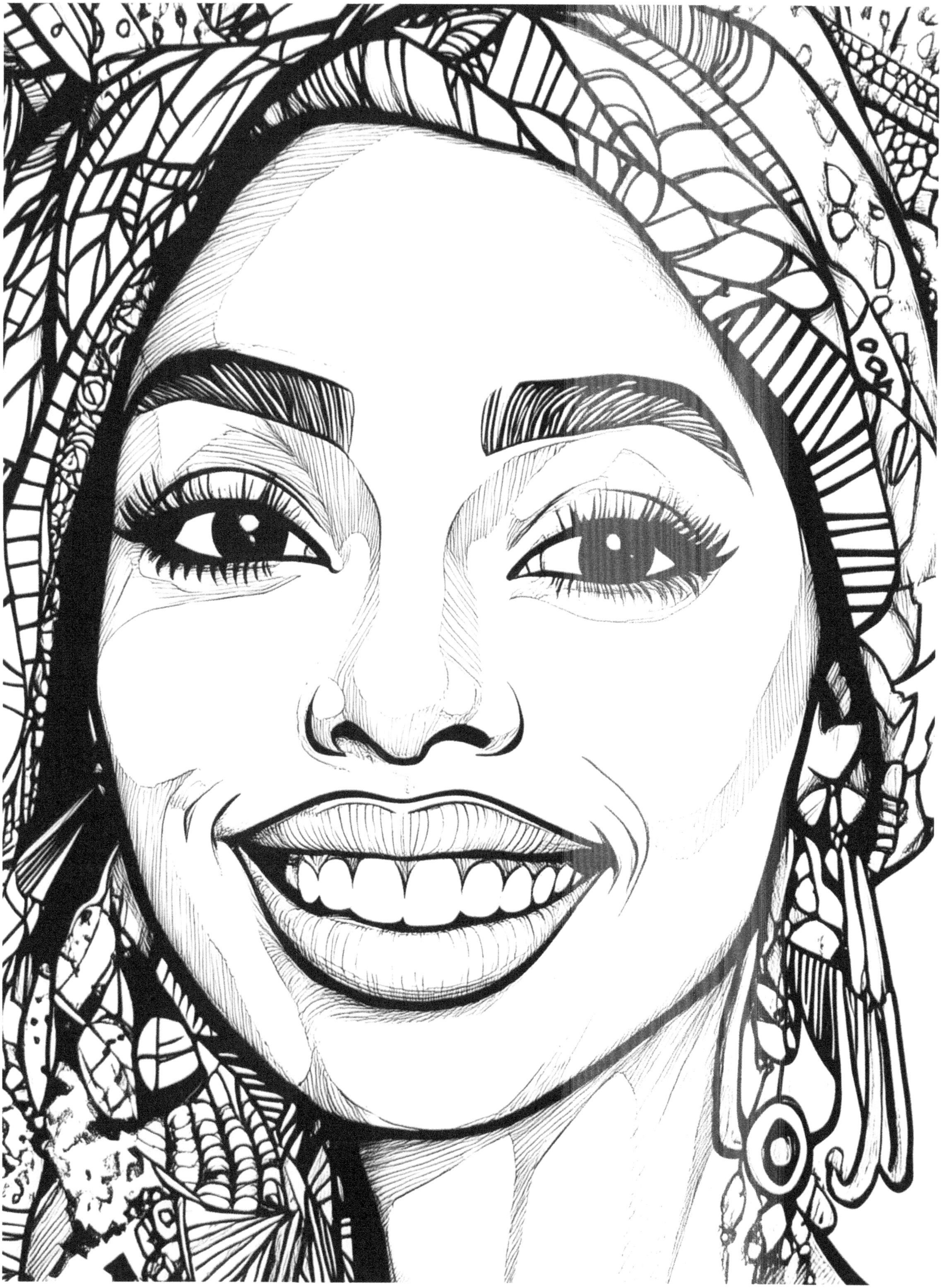

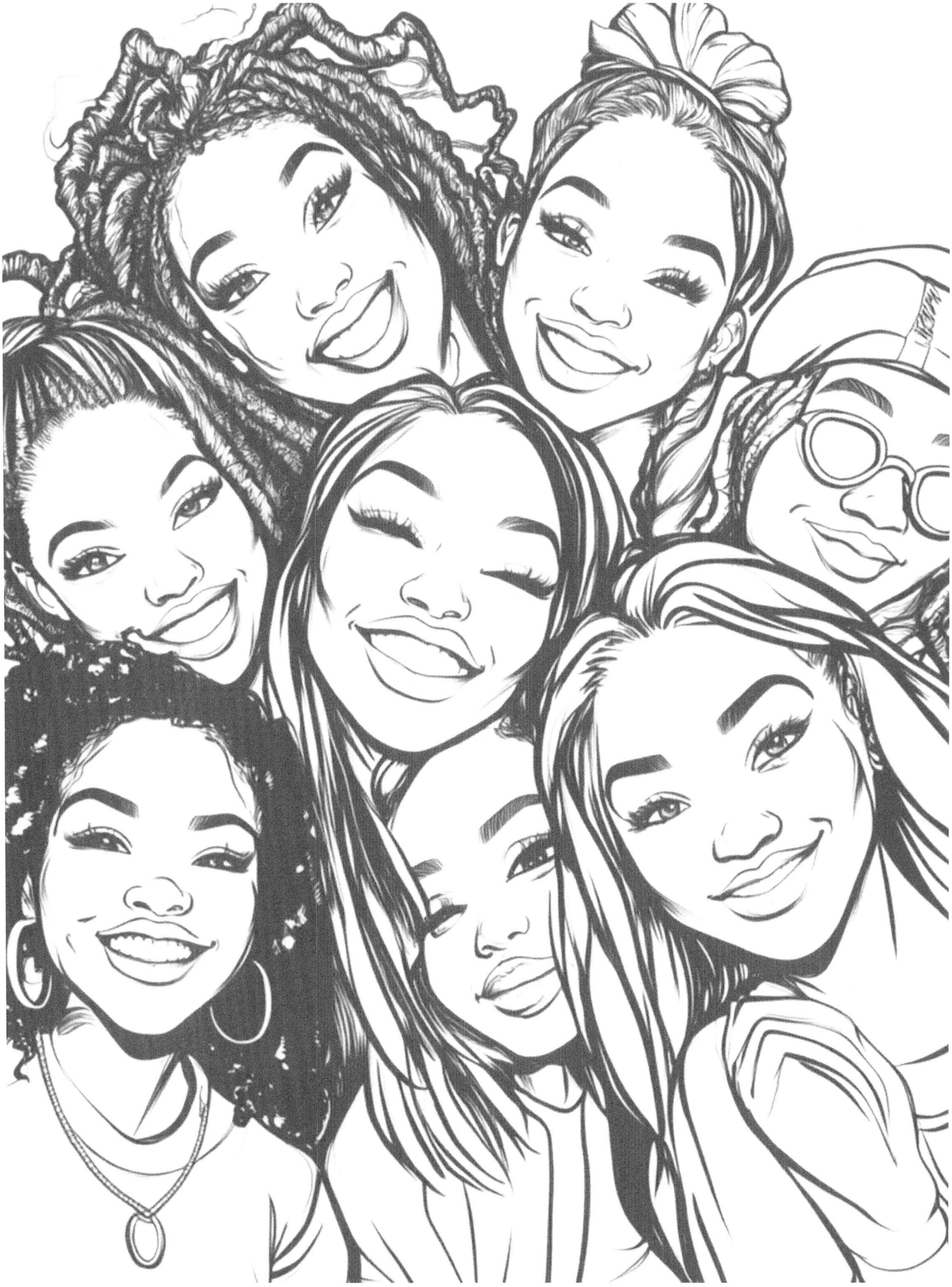

Made in the USA
Middletown, DE
08 November 2024

Made in the USA
Columbia, SC
13 March 2025